Big Fat Hen
and the
Hairy Goat

Vivian French · Jan Lewis

David&Charles
Children's Books

"Cock-a-doodle-doo!"

Red Rooster crowed. "Time to get up!"

"Cluck cluck cluck!"

Big Fat Hen shook her feathers and hurried out of the henhouse. "I must see what needs doing today!"

Outside, Wise Old Dog was lying in the sunshine.
"Good morning, Big Fat Hen," he said.
"Would you have a warm brown egg I
could eat for my breakfast?"

"No, no, no!" clucked Big Fat Hen.
"I'm MUCH too busy to lay eggs."
And she bustled off round the farmyard.

"**Cluck cluck cluck!**
Spotty Pig, are you well?"
"Oink," said Spotty Pig,
and he went on rootling.

"**Cluck cluck cluck!** Brown Cow. Are you well?"

"**Moo,**" said Brown Cow, and she went on chewing.

"**Cluck cluck cluck,** Hairy Goat. Are you well?"

"**Meh,**" said Hairy Goat. "No, I'd like a juicy green cabbage for my breakfast, I'm hungry!"

"**Cluck** cluck **cluck!**" said Big Fat Hen.
"Don't worry, Hairy Goat. I will help you!"

"**Cluck cluck cluck**," said Big Fat Hen, as she hurried off to look for a juicy green cabbage.

"Spotty Pig, Spotty Pig, do you have a juicy green cabbage?"

"**Oink**," said Spotty Pig.
"If I had a juicy green cabbage I'd eat it myself!"

"Brown Cow, Brown Cow, do you have a juicy green cabbage?"

"Moo," said Brown Cow. "If I had a juicy green cabbage I'd eat it myself!"

"Wise Old Dog, Wise Old Dog, do you have a juicy green cabbage?" asked Big Fat Hen.

"Woof!" said Wise Old Dog.
"There are cabbages in Farmer Tile's garden.
Why do you want one?"

Big Fat Hen didn't answer. She was hurrying away
to Farmer Tile's garden. On the other side of the
gate she saw rows and rows of juicy green cabbages.

"Cluck cluck cluck!" she said.
"What a helpful Big Fat Hen I am!"

"Hairy Goat! Hairy Goat!
I have found you LOTS of
juicy green cabbages!"

"But Big Fat Hen," said Hairy Goat, "I can't open the gate."
"Don't worry, Hairy Goat," said Big Fat Hen. "I will help you."
And she flew up to the latch of the gate and opened it wide.

"Meh! Meh! Meh! Breakfast!" said Hairy Goat,
as he hurried into Farmer Tile's garden.

Munch! Munch! Munch!
Hairy Goat gobbled up a juicy green cabbage.

"OINK! Oink! Oink! Breakfast!"
said Spotty Pig, as he followed Hairy Goat.

Munch! Munch! Munch!
Spotty Pig gobbled up two
juicy green cabbages.

"Moo! Moo! Moo! Breakfast!"
said Brown Cow, as she followed Spotty Pig.
Munch! Munch! Munch!
Brown Cow gobbled up three juicy green cabbages.

"**Cluck** cluck cluck! STOP STOP
STOP!" cried Big Fat Hen.
But Hairy Goat and Spotty Pig and
Brown Cow didn't stop.
They went on munching.

Big Fat Hen flapped and clucked, and clucked
and flapped, all the way back to the farmyard.
"Wise Old Dog! Wise Old Dog!
Hairy Goat and Spotty Pig and Brown Cow
are eating ALL Farmer Tile's juicy green cabbages!"

Cluck
Cluck

"Well, well, well," said Wise Old Dog, and he scratched his ear. "I suppose I could chase them out." Big Fat Hen jumped up and down.

"But," said Wise Old Dog, scratching his other ear,
"I haven't had MY breakfast yet . . . And what I really
fancy is a warm brown egg."

Cluck Cluck

"**Cluck** cluck **cluck!**"

"I'll lay you one AT ONCE!"
said Big Fat Hen.

Cluck

Cluck

Cluck

Cluck

So, Wise Old Dog chased Hairy Goat
and Spotty Pig and Brown Cow out
of Farmer Tile's garden . . .
and he slammed the gate shut behind them.

Then he went back to the farmyard to eat his egg.

"**Cluck** cluck **cluck,**" said Big Fat Hen to
herself as she sat at her henhouse door.
"All's well that ends well. Hairy Goat has had his breakfast.
And Spotty Pig. And Brown Cow. And now Wise Old Dog
has had his breakfast too.
What a HELPFUL Big Fat Hen I am!"

E
FRE

First published in Great Britain in 1999 by David and Charles Children's Books.
Winchester House, 259-269 Old Marylebone Road. London NW1 5XJ

2 4 6 8 10 9 7 5 3 1

Text copyright © Vivian French 1999
Illustrations copyright © Jan Lewis 1999

The rights of Vivian French and Jan Lewis to be identified as the
author and illustrator of this work have been asserted by them in
accordance with the Copyright, Designs and Patents Act 1988.

ISBN 1 86233 000 X

A CIP catalogue record for this title is available from the British Library.

Printed in Italy